For Francesca

First published in hardback by Campbell Books in 1995.
This paperback edition published 1996 by Campbell Books,
an imprint of Macmillan Children's Books,
a division of Macmillan Limited,
25 Eccleston Place, London SW1W 9NF
and Basingstoke.

Associated companies throughout the world.

ISBN 0 333 63340 7

A CIP catalogue for this book is available from the British Library.

Printed in Singapore

Little Bird

Rod Campbell

CAMPBELL BOOKS

Little Bird sat in her nest.
Along came a . . .

'I can roar and growl – *you* can't!'
Little Bird felt sad.

Along came a . . .

'I can swing from trees – *you* can't!'
Little Bird felt sad.

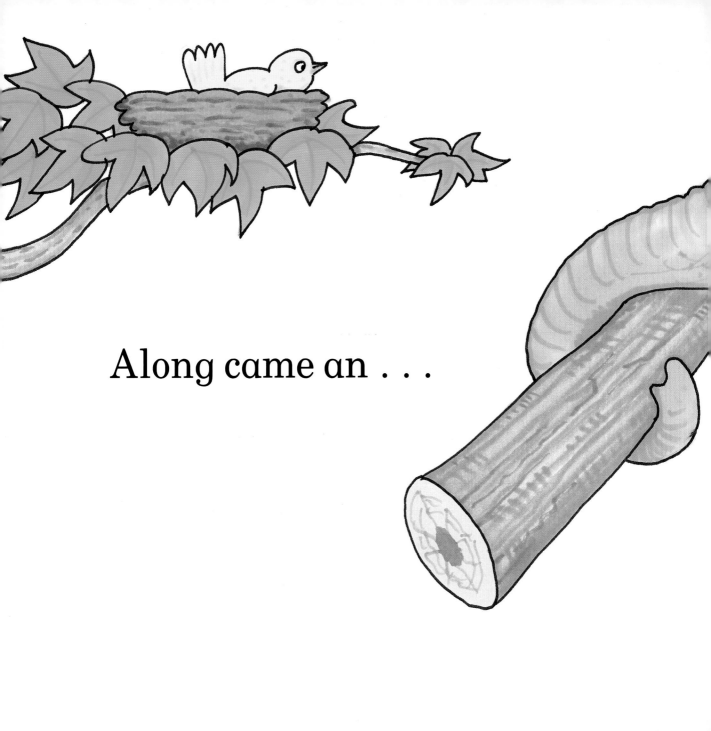

Along came an . . .

'I can lift heavy things – *you* can't!'
Little Bird felt sad.

Along came a . . .

'I can slide through grass – *you* can't!'
Little Bird felt sad.

Along came a . . .

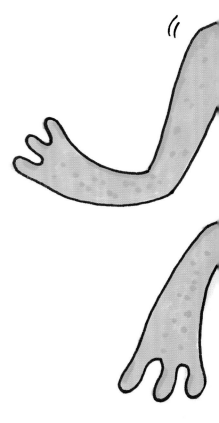

'I can jump over a log – *you* can't!'
Little Bird felt sad.

Along came a . . .

'I can spin a web – *you* can't!'
Little Bird felt sad.

Then Little Bird thought,
'But I've got wings . . .

. . . and I can **fly!**'

She flew up high,
high in the sky.